NCC-1701
GW01607026

Published in Great Britain by Stafford Pemberton Publishing Ltd.,
The Ruskin Chambers, Drury Lane, Knutsford, Cheshire WA16 6HA
Printed and bound in Italy.
ISBN 0 86030 350 0

ANNUAL 1983

STAR TREK
To ERR is
VULCAN
THE INTELLECTUAL ACHIEVEMENTS OF MR.SPOCK ARE LEGENDARY THROUGHOUT THE UNITED FEDERATION OF PLANETS...AND BEYOND! BUT WHEN THAT GREAT MIND SUDDENLY TURNS FOOLISH, THE DANGER IS BEYOND RECKONING!

I TELL YOU, DR. RDAL, I'D STAKE MY REPUTATION ON THIS! A TORNADO IS ABOUT TO FLATTEN THIS ENTIRE CITY!
NO, MR. SPOCK, IT IS MY REPUTATION YOU HAVE STAKED...AND YOU HAVE DESTROYED IT!
THAT'S ENOUGH, MR. SPOCK! YOU WILL REPORT BACK TO THE ENTERPRISE AND REMAIN THERE... UNTIL FURTHER ORDERS!
WRITER-ARNOLD DRAKE
ART- A. McWILLIAMS

CAPTAIN'S LOG: STARDATE 9126.1
Have ordered briefing on next assignment for 0700 hours, ship's time...
...IT'S A PROTOCOL VISIT TO NJURA, THE LARGEST PLANET IN THIS STAR SYSTEM!
MR. SPOCK, WOULD YOU FLIP ON THE HOLO-GRAPHIC PROJECTORS?

INSTANTLY, THE MOST REALISTIC OF IMAGES COMES SHIMMERING TO LIFE!
NJURA WAS THE COLONIAL MASTER OF FOUR OTHER WORLDS FOR NEARLY 1,000 YEARS...FINALLY, ONE REBELLION SUCCEEDED!

STILL ANOTHER NEAR-REAL IMAGE FLASHES ON...
REBELS ON THE OTHER WORLDS WERE ENCOURAGED... THEY CAPTURED MAJOR WEAPONS...
BLOODY PATRIOTIC UPRISINGS BEGAN TO DRAIN THE EMPIRE DRY!

IN THE END, KRING, THEIR EMPEROR, WAS FORCED TO WITHDRAW HIS TROOPS AND SIGN A TREATY OF PEACE AND DISARMAMENT!

THEN, AS THE IMAGES END...
THE EMPEROR IS NOW ELECTED PRESIDENT AND, BY ALL REPORTS, NJURA IS A TRULY PEACE-LOVING WORLD!
ONE OF DEMOCRACY'S GREAT SUCCESS STORIES, EH?

A BIT TOO SUCCESSFUL, IT WOULD SEEM! ANY SUCH SOCIAL UPHEAVAL WOULD REQUIRE MUCH PAINFUL CHANGE!
I DIDN'T SAY IT WAS EASY, MR. SPOCK! THE COLONIAL WARS LASTED FOR A GENERATION AND WERE BRUTAL!

DON'T WASTE YOUR BREATH, JIM! MR. SPOCK CAN NEVER BE CONVINCED THAT THERE IS HOPE FOR US VIOLENT MORTALS!
NOT SO, DR. McCOY! THE HISTORY OF MY OWN PEOPLE REFUTES THAT! VULCANS WERE NOT BORN PEACE LOVING!

AFTER THOUSANDS OF YEARS OF SENSELESS, BLOODY WARS, WE REPLACED BLIND EMOTION WITH COOL REASON!
AH, YES, HERE WE GO AGAIN... "PEACE TREATY MEETING GOING ON INSIDE! PLEASE CHECK YOUR HEART AT THE DOOR"!

CRUDELY PUT, YET ACCURATE... REMOVING EMOTION ELIMINATES HATE AND ITS INEVITABLE COMPANION... WAR!
ALSO ELIMINATING LOVE, COMPASSION AND DECENCY! WELCOME TO MR. SPOCK'S ROBOT WORLD!

IN THE TRANSPORTER ROOM...

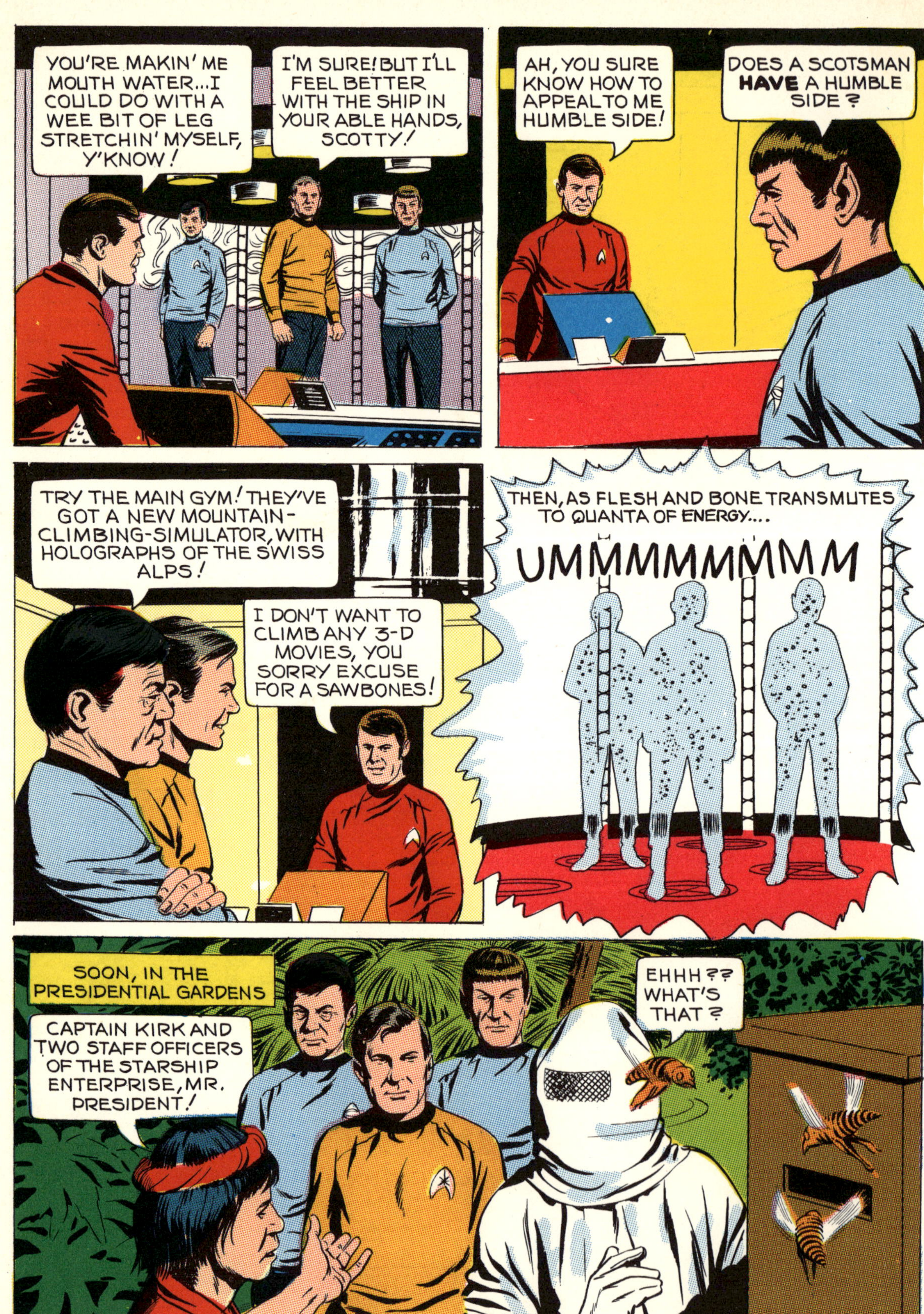
YOU'RE MAKIN' ME MOUTH WATER...I COULD DO WITH A WEE BIT OF LEG STRETCHIN' MYSELF, Y'KNOW!
I'M SURE! BUT I'LL FEEL BETTER WITH THE SHIP IN YOUR ABLE HANDS, SCOTTY!
AH, YOU SURE KNOW HOW TO APPEAL TO ME HUMBLE SIDE!
DOES A SCOTSMAN **HAVE** A HUMBLE SIDE?
TRY THE MAIN GYM! THEY'VE GOT A NEW MOUNTAIN-CLIMBING-SIMULATOR, WITH HOLOGRAPHS OF THE SWISS ALPS!
I DON'T WANT TO CLIMB ANY 3-D MOVIES, YOU SORRY EXCUSE FOR A SAWBONES!
THEN, AS FLESH AND BONE TRANSMUTES TO QUANTA OF ENERGY....
UMMMMMMMMM
SOON, IN THE PRESIDENTIAL GARDENS
CAPTAIN KIRK AND TWO STAFF OFFICERS OF THE STARSHIP ENTERPRISE, MR. PRESIDENT!
EHHH?? WHAT'S THAT?

OH, YES, OF COURSE... WELCOME, GENTLEMEN...
KINDLY FORGIVE THE DIVERSION OF AN OLD MAN... I AM BREEDING A NEW KIND OF BEE!

THROUGH CROSS BREEDING, I HAVE PRODUCED A SUPERB VARIETY OF... VARTA... I BELIEVE YOU CALL IT, "HONEY"!
THAT IS ENORMOUS! MAY I INSPECT IT?

NEVER WITHOUT PROTECTIVE CLOTHING! ITS POISON IS DEADLY... THE STING EXCRUCIATING!
NOT TO MR. SPOCK, I SUSPECT! VULCANS DON'T FEEL ANYTHING!

LATER, OVER THE NJURIAN EQUIVALENT OF TEA...
YOU'RE EARLY FOR OUR CELEBRATION, BUT THERE IS MUCH FOR YOU TO SEE EVEN NOW!
THIS DELICATE, PINK, CREAMY SUBSTANCE IN THE CAKES... IS THAT VARTA?

YES... MOST OBSERVANT OF YOU, MR. SPOCK... NOW... WHAT WOULD YOU CARE TO SEE FIRST?
ONE OF YOUR HOSPITALS!
A PHYSICAL SCIENCE CENTER!
A SPACE NAVIGATION SCHOOL!

A MIXED MENU! BUT I BELIEVE WE CAN SATISFY ALL APPETITES! TJARK, SUMMON DR. M.H. RDAL!
YES, MR. PRESIDENT!

MINUTES LATER...
GENTLEMEN, DR. MLANY RDAL IS A LEADING MIND IN THREE MAJOR SCIENCES AND ABLY FITTED TO GUIDE YOU!
MORE THAN PLEASED, DR. RDAL!

DO ANY OF YOU UNDERSTAND THE 3RD FIELD THEORY OF ADVANCED PHYSICS?
WE ALL DO, BUT WE CALL IT "POST EINSTEINIAN-3"! MR. SPOCK IS SOMETHING OF AN EXPERT IN IT!

WHAT ABOUT ELECTRO-BIONICS?
I HAD 12 CREDITS IN IT AT THE ACADEMY BUT MR. SPOCK HAS DONE SPECIAL READING IN THAT AREA, TOO!

WHAT ABOUT OUR WORK IN PEACEFUL USES OF SUB-ATOMIC ENERGY? ARE YOU INTERESTED?
HI-N ION STREAMS AND THE LIKE? ANY STAR-SHIP COMMANDER WOULD BE...AND, AGAIN, MR. SPOCK HAS DONE POST-GRAD WORK THERE!

THIS ENTIRE TOUR SHOULD BE OF SPECIAL INTEREST TO YOU, MR. SPOCK! YOU POSSESS A MOST PROTEAN INTELLECT!
THE DOCTOR SEEMS MORE THAN A BIT DRAWN TO MR. SPOCK!

TO REALLY SCRAMBLE A METAPHOR, THE LADY IS BARKING UP THE WRONG ICEBERG...
ON A SCALE OF '10', MR. SPOCK'S EMOTIONS HAVE YET TO HIT '1'!

LATER, AT THE GIANT GENERATOR PLANT...
ELEVEN OF THESE MAMMOTH NUCLEAR "OVENS" DEVELOP ENOUGH ELECTRICITY FOR OUR ENTIRE WORLD!
HOW SAFE ARE THEY?
THERE ARE 72 FAIL-SAFE DEVICES BUILT IN! THERE IS **NOT ONE** RECORDED ACCIDENT IN RECENT HISTORY!

THE ENERGY IS RADIOED TO SATELLITES FOR DISTRIBUTION TO A WIDE AREA THROUGH CLEARLY MARKED HIGH-ENERGY CHANNELS!
ELIMINATING LONG-HAUL CABLES AND THE LOSS OF ENERGY THROUGH SUCH CARRIERS! YES, WE USE QUITE THE SAME SYSTEM!

AND, AS THE TOUR CONTINUES...
THIS IS THE CONTROL CENTER FOR THE ENTIRE PLANT! EVERY DROP OF ENERGY DEVELOPED AND TRANSMITTED FROM HERE IS CAREFULLY MONITORED BY COMPUTER!

THE COMPUTER IS ABLE TO COORDINATE ALL THE DATA AND ANTICIPATE THE SLIGHTEST DANGER LONG BEFORE IT CAN PRESENT A RISK!
HMMM... I WONDER!

WHAT'S THAT, MR. SP.....
QUIET, PLEASE, DOCTOR...I AM DOUBLE-CHECKING MY CALCULATIONS!

BUT WHAT....
YES!...I'M CERTAIN OF IT NOW! PLEASE, DR. RDAL, YOU MUST CLOSE DOWN GENERATORS 5 AND 6! THEY ARE APPROACHING A CRITICAL CONDITION!
WHAT??

PREPOSTEROUS! NO GENERATOR COULD EVEN APPROACH CRITICAL WITHOUT A DOZEN ALARMS SOUNDING!
I TELL YOU, I'VE RECHECKED MY CALCULATIONS...

HALF YOUR PLANET WILL BE OBLITERATED UNLESS YOU CLOSE DOWN THOSE TWO NUKE-GENS AT ONCE!
AND I TELL YOU, YOU'RE ABSOLUTELY WRONG!

"WRONG" IS A WORD THAT MR. SPOCK HAS NEVER HEARD APPLIED TO HIM-SELF! YOU MAY HAVE TO TRANSLATE IT FOR HIM, DOCTOR!
I CAN SEE THAT MY WORDS ARE WASTED HERE!

AND, WITHOUT ANOTHER WORD, MR. SPOCK FLINGS HIMSELF INTO ACTION...
CRZZZ
CRZZZ
IF MY CALCULATIONS ARE CORRECT, THESE ARE THE MAIN CIRCUIT BREAKERS FOR GENERATORS FIVE AND SIX!

YOU'VE JUST DENIED ELECTRICAL POWER TO 100 MILLION PEOPLE!
WITH CAUSE... I'LL STAKE MY REPUTATION ON IT!
AND OURS AS WELL, MR. SPOCK!
END OF PART I

"IMPERVIOUS TO THE ILLOGICAL"

WORDSEARCH
SULU
COMBAT
SPOCK
SHUTTLECRA
JAMES
SCOTTY
COMPUTER
VULCAN
COSMOS
GALAXY

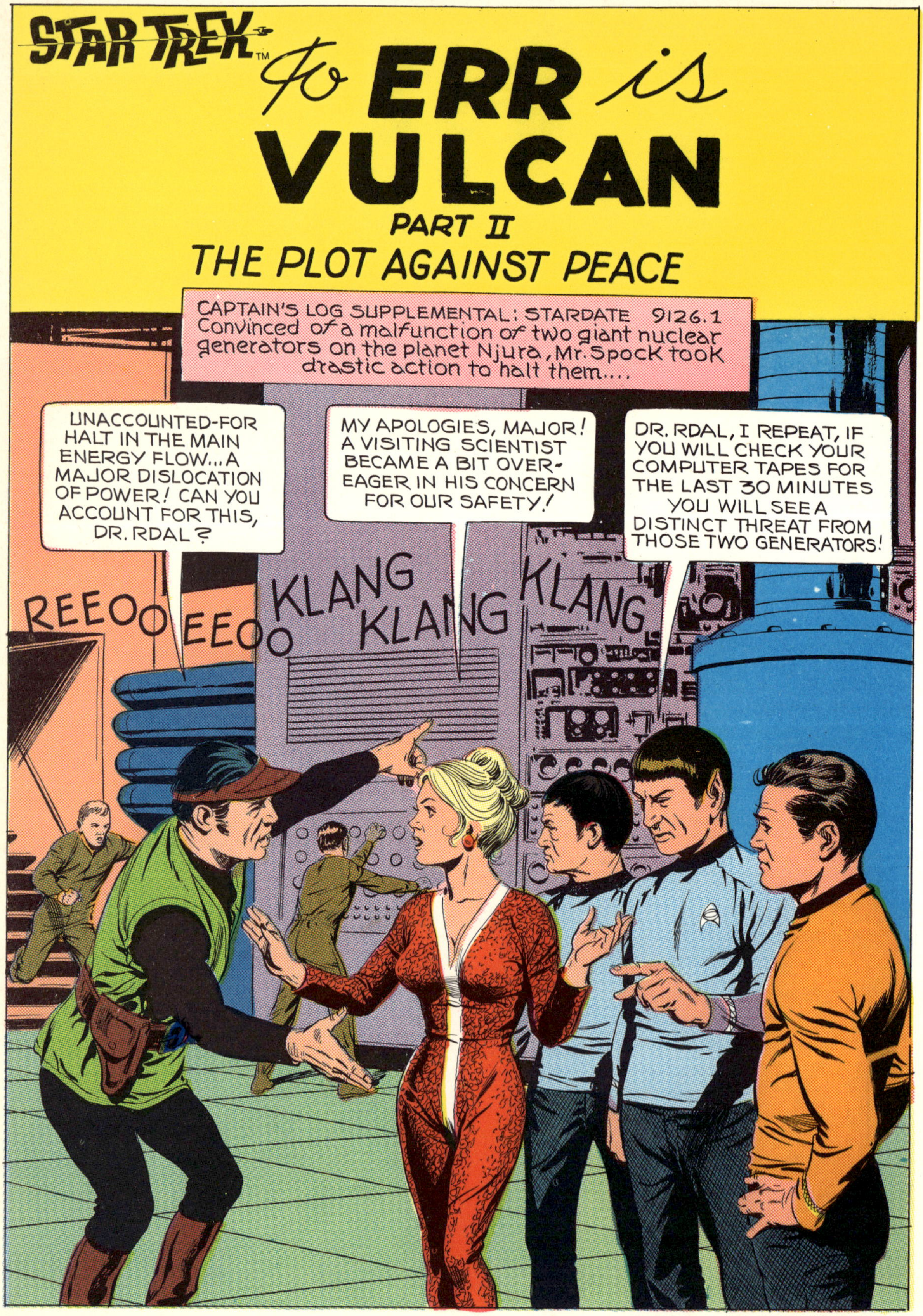

PART II
THE PLOT AGAINST PEACE

CAPTAIN'S LOG SUPPLEMENTAL: STARDATE 9126.1
Convinced of a malfunction of two giant nuclear generators on the planet Njura, Mr. Spock took drastic action to halt them....

UNACCOUNTED-FOR HALT IN THE MAIN ENERGY FLOW...A MAJOR DISLOCATION OF POWER! CAN YOU ACCOUNT FOR THIS, DR. RDAL?

MY APOLOGIES, MAJOR! A VISITING SCIENTIST BECAME A BIT OVER-EAGER IN HIS CONCERN FOR OUR SAFETY!

DR. RDAL, I REPEAT, IF YOU WILL CHECK YOUR COMPUTER TAPES FOR THE LAST 30 MINUTES YOU WILL SEE A DISTINCT THREAT FROM THOSE TWO GENERATORS!

REEOOOEEOO

KLANG KLANG KLANG

I TELL YOU, BOTH GENERATORS WERE WITHIN TWO OR THREE MINUTES OF CRITICAL MASS!
NONSENSE! THE FIRST FAIL-SAFE WARNINGS WOULD HAVE SOUNDED HOURS AGO AND SHUT DOWN **EVERYTHING!**

QUICKLY, DR. RDAL "QUESTIONS" THE GREAT DATA CENTER...
THIS VERIFIES THE COMPLETE SAFETY OF EVERY ONE OF THE GENERATORS!
IMPOSSIBLE, I TELL YOU! BUT FOR MY ACTION WE'D HAVE ALL BEEN KILLED! HERE, LET ME DEMONSTRATE!

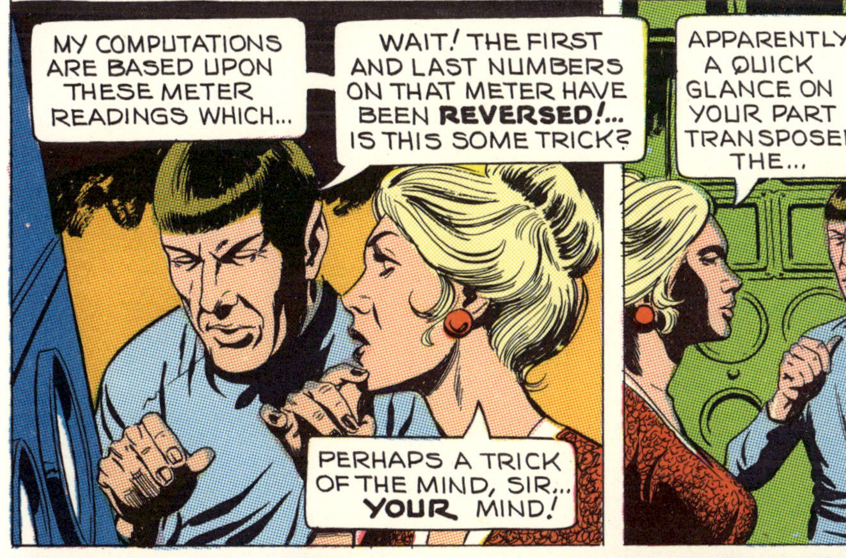
MY COMPUTATIONS ARE BASED UPON THESE METER READINGS WHICH...
WAIT! THE FIRST AND LAST NUMBERS ON THAT METER HAVE BEEN **REVERSED!**... IS THIS SOME TRICK?
PERHAPS A TRICK OF THE MIND, SIR... **YOUR** MIND!

APPARENTLY, A QUICK GLANCE ON YOUR PART TRANSPOSED THE...
I DO NOT MAKE SIMPLE, CARELESS ERRORS OF THAT NATURE!
HOW DID I KNOW HE WOULD SAY THAT, JIM?

ASTOUNDING AS YOUR INTELLECT IS, EVEN **YOU** CAN MAKE AN ERROR! BUT TRY TO RESTRAIN YOURSELF ON THE REST OF OUR TOUR!
I SIMPLY DO NOT UNDERSTAND IT!
IF I DIDN'T KNOW IT TO BE IMPOSSIBLE, I'D SAY THAT MR. SPOCK IS BLUSHING!

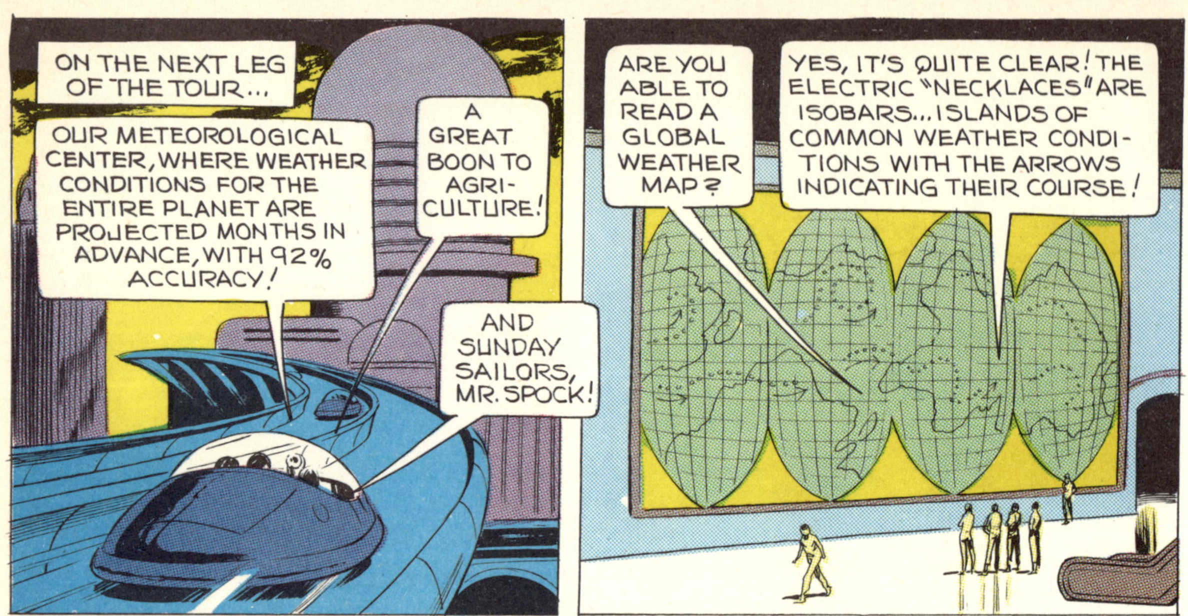
ON THE NEXT LEG OF THE TOUR...
OUR METEOROLOGICAL CENTER, WHERE WEATHER CONDITIONS FOR THE ENTIRE PLANET ARE PROJECTED MONTHS IN ADVANCE, WITH 92% ACCURACY!
A GREAT BOON TO AGRI-CULTURE!
AND SUNDAY SAILORS, MR. SPOCK!
ARE YOU ABLE TO READ A GLOBAL WEATHER MAP?
YES, IT'S QUITE CLEAR! THE ELECTRIC "NECKLACES" ARE ISOBARS... ISLANDS OF COMMON WEATHER CONDI-TIONS WITH THE ARROWS INDICATING THEIR COURSE!

OUR ROOFTOP OBSERVATORY IS WORTH A LOOK... JOIN US, MR. SPOCK?
IN A MOMENT... I WANT ANOTHER LOOK AT THIS FASCINATING MAP!

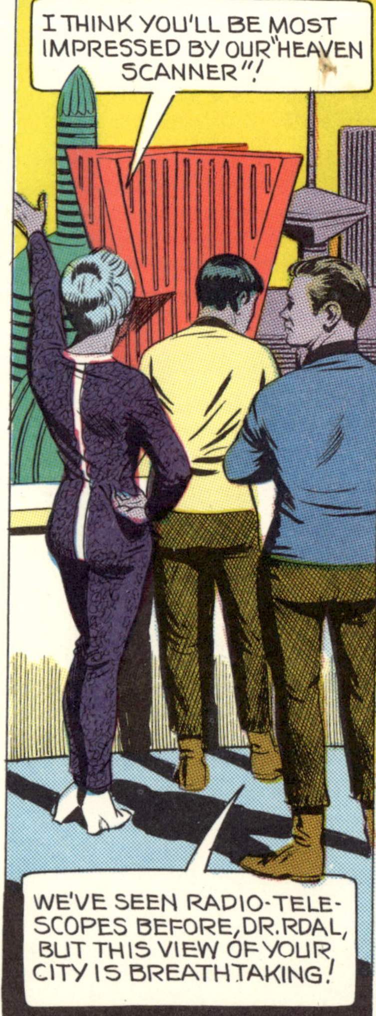
I THINK YOU'LL BE MOST IMPRESSED BY OUR "HEAVEN SCANNER"!
WE'VE SEEN RADIO-TELE-SCOPES BEFORE, DR. RDAL, BUT THIS VIEW OF YOUR CITY IS BREATHTAKING!

DR. RDAL! AT THE RISK OF BEING THOUGHT A TOTAL ALARMIST, I MUST WARN YOU THAT THIS CITY IS IN THE DIRECT PATH OF A TORNADO!
NOW, SEE HERE, MR. SPOCK...

I HAVE CHECKED MY COMPUTATIONS THREE TIMES! THERE CAN BE NO DOUBT!
WELL, THIS WILL BE EASY ENOUGH TO CHECK OUT!
OH, BROTHER, NOT AGAIN!

A QUICK CALL TO THE PLOTTING CENTER, AND...
...ABSOLUTELY NO TORNADO CONDITIONS IN THE AREA? IS THAT SO...OH?..INTERESTING! THANK YOU, PROFESSOR KSANTHA!
IMPOSSIBLE! TELL HIM TO CHECK IT OUT AGAIN!

I DON'T LIKE BEING MADE A FOOL OF BEFORE MY COLLEAGUES! I DON'T UNDERSTAND YOUR GAME, MR SPOCK, BUT...
I ASSURE YOU THAT NO "GAME" IS INVOLVED, DOCTOR! DATA FROM YOUR OWN INSTRUMENTS PERMIT NO ALTERNATIVE ANALYSIS! I'LL SHOW YOU...COME!

QUICKLY, THE VULCAN POINTS OUT THE BASIS OF HIS CONCLUSION!
SEE THE VAST PRESSURE DIFFERENCE IN THE ADJOINING ISOBARS? NOW OBSERVE THE DIRECTION IN WHICH BOTH...
WAIT! WHAT TERRIBLE JOKE IS BEING PLAYED HERE?

ONE OF THOSE DIRECTIONAL ARROWS HAS BEEN **REVERSED**!
I THOUGHT YOU MIGHT SAY THAT! PROFESSOR KSANTHA SAID, "EXCEPT FOR ONE OF THOSE DIRECTIONS, YOUR ALARM WOULD BE JUSTIFIED"! ANOTHER "SMALL ERROR" IN OBSERVATION, MR. SPOCK!

AT THE MOMENT I COULD BE DOING SOME IMPORTANT RESEARCH...THEREFORE, YOUR JOKES DO NOT AMU...
I MUST ASSURE-
I ALREADY HAVE HAD **TWO** OF YOUR ASSURANCES, MR. SPOCK!

MR. SPOCK, I BELIEVE OUR MISSION WILL BEST BE SERVED IF YOU RETURN TO THE SHIP!
SAY, JIM, THAT'S PRETTY STIFF! ANYONE CAN MAKE A MISTAKE!

CAN MR. SPOCK MAKE **TWO** BASIC ERRORS WITHOUT SOMETHING BEING VERY WRONG?
PLACE YOURSELF IN THE SICK BAY! DR. McCOY WILL EXAMINE YOU ON OUR RETURN!
YES, CAPTAIN!

AT THE COMMAND, "BEAM UP," A FORLORN MR. SPOCK VANISHES!
I...I HATE TO THINK I WAS INSTRUMENTAL IN HIS HUMILIATION!
I COULDN'T WAIT FOR THE DAY SPOCK WOULD BE HUMBLED! NOW IT'S HERE AND... I FEEL TERRIBLE!

I WOULD PREFER NOT TO CONTINUE THIS TOUR! YOU WILL BE ESCORTED TO YOUR HOTEL! I WILL CALL FOR YOU IN THE MORNING!
THANK YOU, DOCTOR... WE UNDERSTAND!

LATER, AS THEY PROCEED BY ELECTROCAR...
JIM, WHAT ABOUT THE POSSIBILITY THAT SPOCK WAS SET UP?
I'VE THOUGHT OF THAT, BUT IT MAKES NO SENSE! ENEMIES ON A WORLD HE'S NEVER SET FOOT ON BEFORE?...NOT LIKELY!

NO! THE ONLY REASON WE BOTH CONSIDERED SUCH A WILD NOTION IS THAT WE THINK OF SPOCK AS INTELLECTUAL PERFECTION...
BUT **NOBODY** IS THAT! THE LAWS OF CHANCE CAUGHT UP WITH HIM... **TWICE!**

AT THE HOTEL...
STILL, YOU COULD HAVE SIMPLY WARNED HIM...
DR. RDAL HAD BEEN HUMILIATED BEFORE A FELLOW SCIENTIST! I HAD TO SAVE HER FACE...BY KICKING SPOCK'S POSTERIOR... DO YOU THINK I **ENJOYED** THAT?

THE FOLLOWING DAWN...
WAKE UP, YOU SLEEPY-HEADS! THE PEACE ANNIVERSARY PARADE IS ABOUT TO BEGIN!
BE WITH YOU IN A FEW MINUTES, DOCTOR!

COME ON! WE'LL MISS THE OPENING DISPLAY!
I JUST WANT TO MAKE SURE I'VE GOT MY BOOTS ON THE RIGHT FEET!

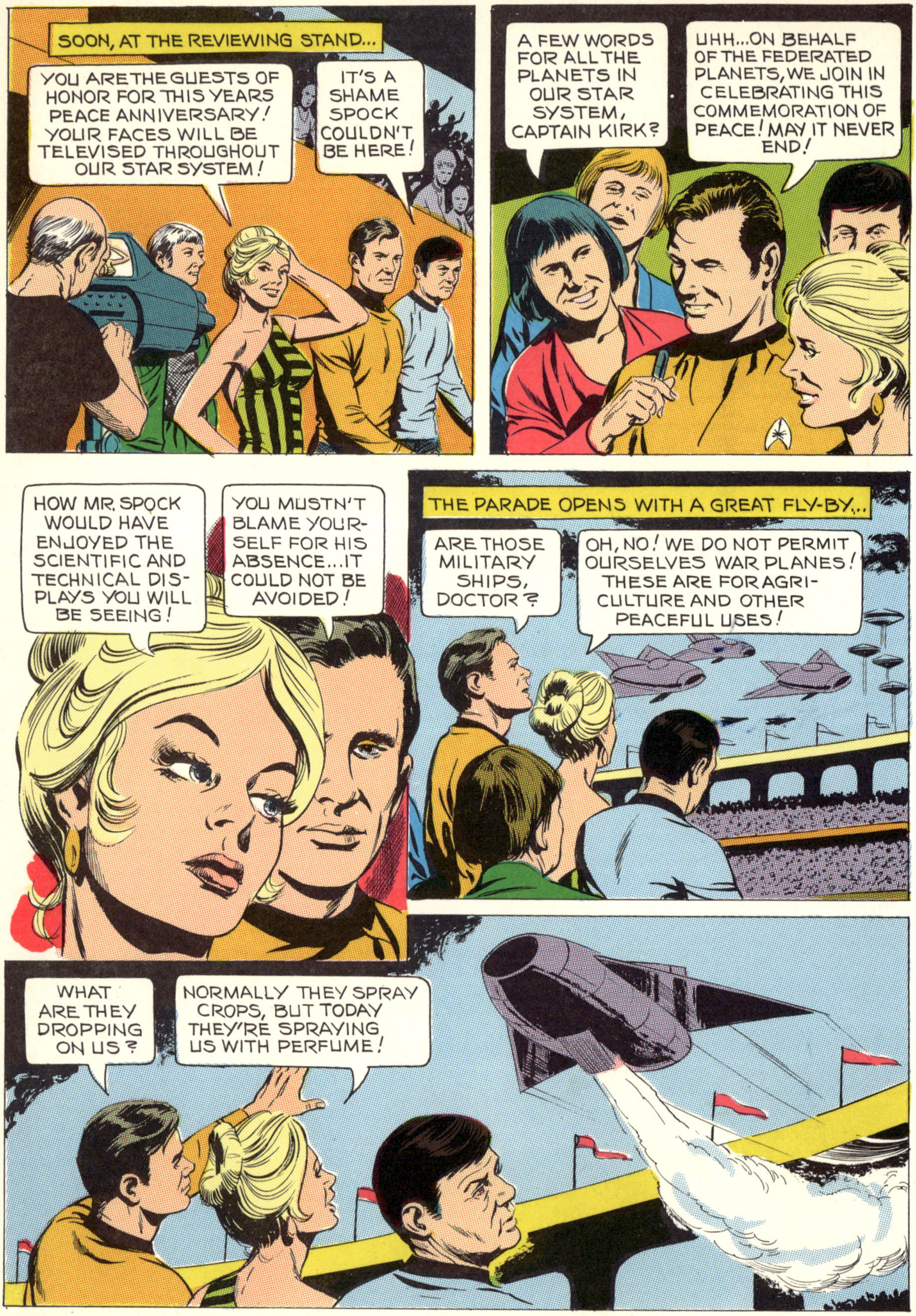

HOW MR. SPOCK WOULD HAVE ENJOYED THE SCIENTIFIC AND TECHNICAL DISPLAYS YOU WILL BE SEEING!

YOU MUSTN'T BLAME YOURSELF FOR HIS ABSENCE...IT COULD NOT BE AVOIDED!

THE PARADE OPENS WITH A GREAT FLY-BY...

ARE THOSE MILITARY SHIPS, DOCTOR?

OH, NO! WE DO NOT PERMIT OURSELVES WAR PLANES! THESE ARE FOR AGRICULTURE AND OTHER PEACEFUL USES!

WHAT ARE THEY DROPPING ON US?

NORMALLY THEY SPRAY CROPS, BUT TODAY THEY'RE SPRAYING US WITH PERFUME!

THEN A GIANT TV SCREEN COMES TO LIFE!
LOOK UP THERE, JIM! YOU'LL NEVER SEE A BIGGER PICTURE OF YOURSELF!
I DON'T THINK I'D WANT TO, BONES! I'M MORE THE HOLO-SNAP TYPE MYSELF!

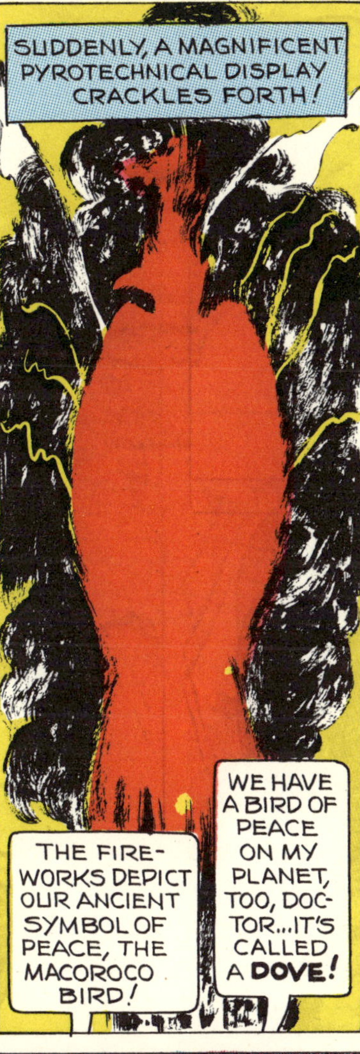
SUDDENLY, A MAGNIFICENT PYROTECHNICAL DISPLAY CRACKLES FORTH!
THE FIRE-WORKS DEPICT OUR ANCIENT SYMBOL OF PEACE, THE MACOROCO BIRD!
WE HAVE A BIRD OF PEACE ON MY PLANET, TOO, DOC-TOR...IT'S CALLED A DOVE!

THESE ARE SOME OF OUR FARMERS! ONCE, THOSE TOOLS WERE RIFLES AND SUCH MEN WERE SOLDIERS!
WELL, THEY MARCH AS WELL AS ANY SOLDIERS I'VE EVER SEEN!

THOSE ARE FARMING COMBINES WHICH DO THE WORK OF HUNDREDS OF MEN! ONCE THEY WOULD HAVE BEEN TANKS!
IT'S A LOT BETTER TO CUT DOWN WHEAT THAN TO CUT DOWN MEN!

AND, AS THE HUGE COMBINES BEGIN TO PARADE AROUND THE STADIUM...
WHAT IN...THE COMBINES.... THEY'RE HEATING UP... STARTING TO **GLOW!!**

THE HEAT INTENSIFIES WITH EACH SECOND...
THE HEAT IS DRIVING THE OPERATORS FROM THEIR SEATS...BUT WHAT'S CAUSING IT?
AH-H-H

THEY'RE **MELTING!**.. BUT ONLY THE OUTER SKIN! SO THE HEAT IS LOCATED SOMEWHERE CLOSE TO THE SURFACE!
I THINK I'M BEGINNING TO SEE THROUGH THIS...**LITERALLY!**

AS THE 'SKINS' OF THE GIANT MACHINES CONTINUE TO MELT...
THEY'RE TANKS, NOT COMBINES! A SUPER-STRUCTURE OF THIN METAL DISGUISED THEM! ALL OF THIS HAS BEEN A SHAM!
THEY'VE BEEN SECRETLY REARMING AGAINST THEIR OLD COLONIES... BUT WHO EXPOSED THE PLOT, JIM?

LOOK!.. DOWN BY THAT ENTRANCE.... THE POLICE SEEM TO HAVE CAPTURED SOMEONE! I MUST GO DOWN THERE!

WE HAVE CAPTURED THE SABOTEUR, MR. PRESIDENT!
HOLD HIM FOR SUMMARY JUDGEMENT! HE'LL LEARN HOW WE DEAL WITH SUCH TREACHERY!
ITS MR. SPOCK!

YOU FORGET, PRESIDENT KRING, THAT YOUR PLOT HAS JUST BEEN EXPOSED TO THE FORMER COLONIES VIA TELEVISION!
SO...YOU UNCOVERED MY PART IN THIS! THEN WE WILL SPEED UP THE TIME-TABLE...THE RECONQUEST SHALL BEGIN AT ONCE!

THAT WILL NOT BE EASY, SIR! YOU SEE, I SECRETLY RE-VISITED THE GREAT POWER PLANT AND THE WEATHER CENTER SOME MINUTES AGO!
YOU... WHAT?

YES, I HAVE SABOTAGED THEM BOTH! WITHOUT GROUND POWER OR WEATHER DATA...
...THERE CAN BE NO INVASION!... I'M **FINISHED!!** IF THE COLONIALS DON'T KILL ME, MY OWN MILITARY WILL!

IT DOESN'T HAVE TO BE THAT WAY... PROVIDED YOU'VE LEARNED YOUR LESSON!
YOU THERE, TV TECHNICIAN...BRING YOUR CAMERA WITH US TO THE PRESIDENT'S BOX!

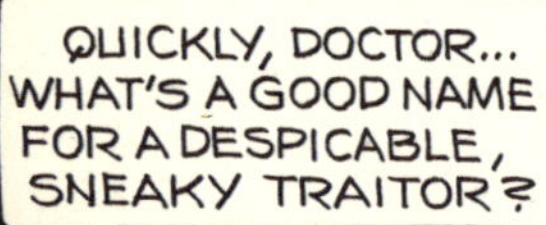
QUICKLY, DOCTOR... WHAT'S A GOOD NAME FOR A DESPICABLE, SNEAKY TRAITOR?

GMAR! IT IS MY YOUNGER BROTHER'S NAME... AND AS A CHILD, HE WAS **ALL** THOSE THINGS!

MOMENTS LATER ON THE BIG STADIUM SCREEN...
A MILITARY PLOT TO REINVADE YOUR BROTHER PLANETS HAS BEEN SMASHED BY PRESIDENT KRING! THE WEAPONS WILL BE PUBLICLY DESTROYED! AUTHORITIES ARE NOW SEEKING...
THE INFAMOUS "GENERAL GMAR", THE RINGLEADER!

HAIL KRING
KEEPER OF THE PEACE!
HE'S NOT THE FIRST LEADER TO TAKE CREDIT FOR THE OPPOSITE OF HIS ACTIONS!
YES, BUT THEY'LL BE WATCHING HIM A LOT CLOSER FROM NOW ON!

LATER, AT THE HOTEL...
KRING'S ADVISERS, KNOWING MR. SPOCK'S REPUTATION, FEARED HE WOULD SEE THROUGH THE "PEACE PARADE"!
SO THEY RIGGED THINGS TO MAKE HIM SEEM TOTALLY UNRELIABLE!

ORDERING HIM BACK TO THE SHIP WAS A TRICK, EH?
YES! IT FREED HIM TO INVESTIGATE THINGS! I COULDN'T EVEN TELL BONES HERE, FOR FEAR WE WERE BEING "TAPPED"!

I WAS CERTAIN THE PEACE PARADE WAS AT THE HEART OF THIS!
WHEN I DISCOVERED THE CAMOUFLAGED TANKS, I PLANTED THERMAL CHARGES THAT WOULD MELT THE LIGHT, OUTER METAL ONLY!

CAN YOU BELIEVE THAT I HAD NOTHING TO DO WITH THIS PLOT AGAINST YOU?
EASILY, DOCTOR... IF ANYONE AS BRILLIANT AS YOU HAD DONE IT, IT MIGHT HAVE SUCCEEDED!

SHORTLY, ABOARD THE ENTERPRISE...
...AND STOP TALKING ABOUT YOUR MANY "MISTAKES"! THERE WERE ONLY TWO!
FOR A VULCAN, DR. McCOY, THAT IS TWO TOO MANY!!
END

RACE THROUGH SPACE

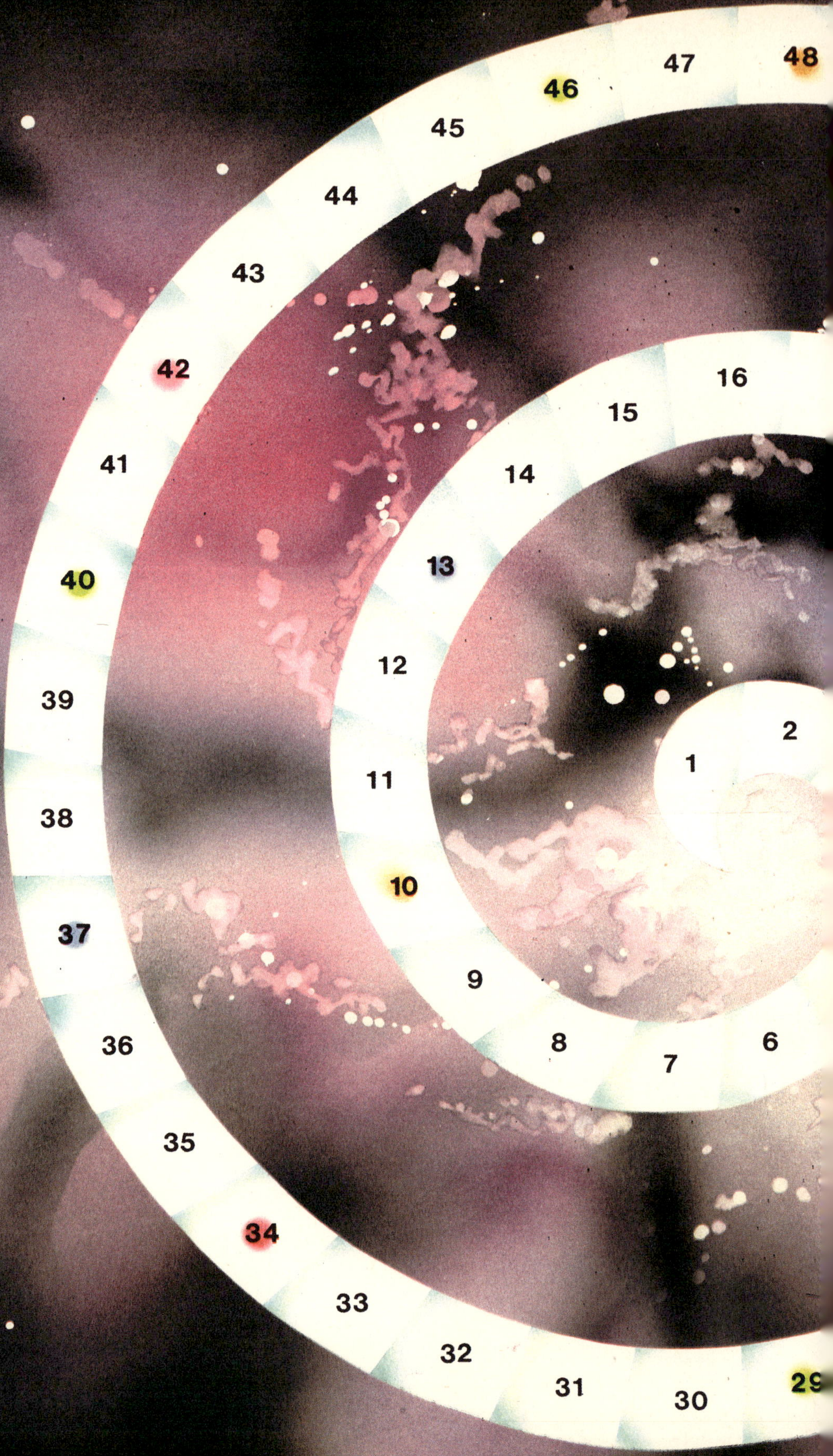

1 2 6 7 8 9 10 11 12 13 14 15 16 29 30 31 32 33 34 35 36 37 38 39 40 41 42 43 44 45 46 47 48

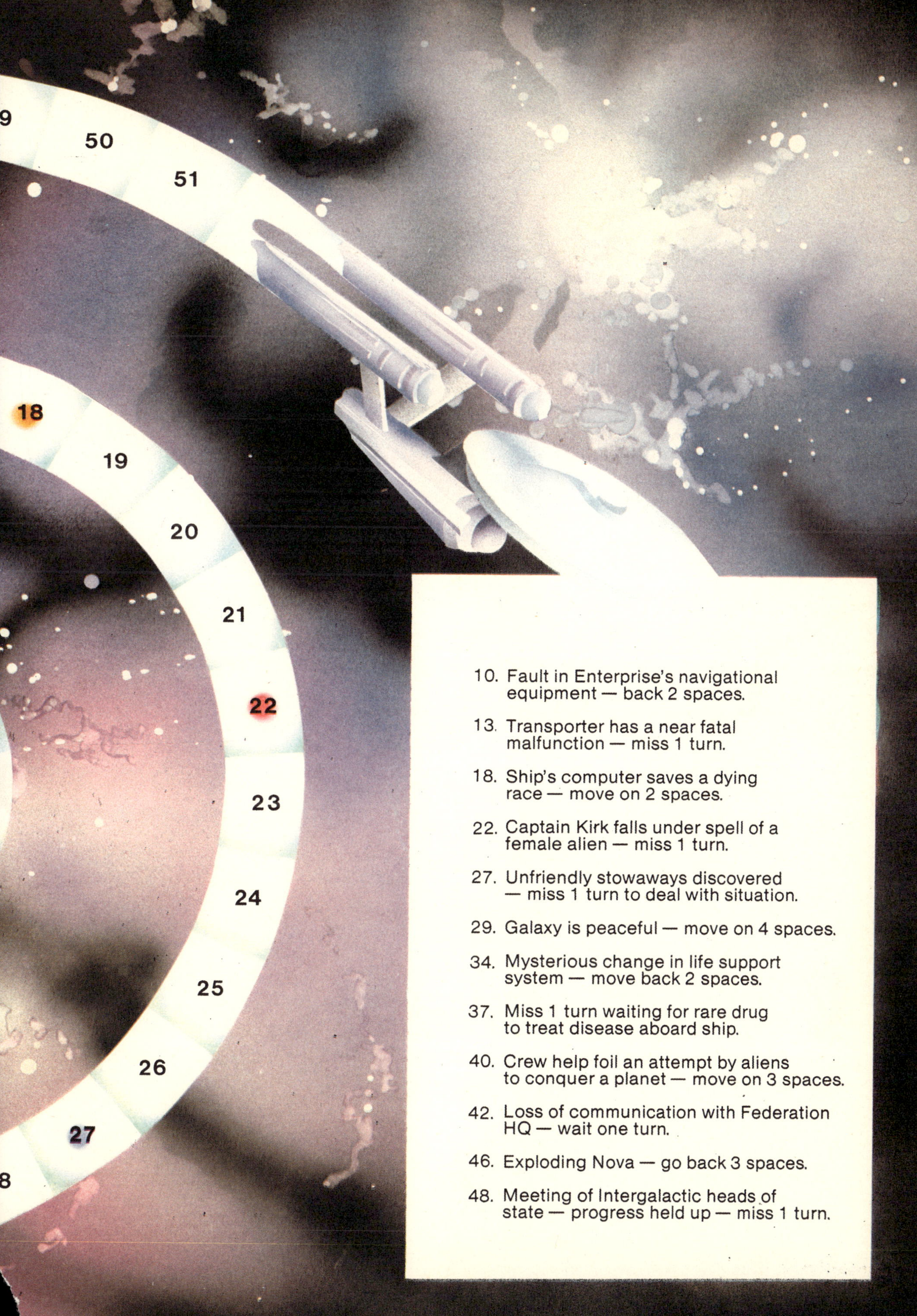

10. Fault in Enterprise's navigational equipment — back 2 spaces.

13. Transporter has a near fatal malfunction — miss 1 turn.

18. Ship's computer saves a dying race — move on 2 spaces.

22. Captain Kirk falls under spell of a female alien — miss 1 turn.

27. Unfriendly stowaways discovered — miss 1 turn to deal with situation.

29. Galaxy is peaceful — move on 4 spaces.

34. Mysterious change in life support system — move back 2 spaces.

37. Miss 1 turn waiting for rare drug to treat disease aboard ship.

40. Crew help foil an attempt by aliens to conquer a planet — move on 3 spaces.

42. Loss of communication with Federation HQ — wait one turn.

46. Exploding Nova — go back 3 spaces.

48. Meeting of Intergalactic heads of state — progress held up — miss 1 turn.

"The Wrath of KHAN"

STAR TREK
OPERATION CON GAME
IT BEGAN AS A PETTY, ALMOST LAUGHABLE CRIME...BUT BEHIND IT WAS A FOE WHOSE CUNNING AND TREACHERY WOULD SWIFTLY LEAD THE GALAXY TO THE BRINK OF WAR!
WRITER: GEORGE KASHDAN
ART: A. McWILLIAMS
WHAT HAPPENED, MR. SCOTT? WHY'D YOU LOSE CONTACT?
I CAN'T SAY, LADDIE... BUT IF CAPTAIN KIRK AND MR. SPOCK WERE CAPTURED ABOARD THAT KLINGON WARSHIP, I WOULDN'T GIVE A SCOTCH FARTHING FOR THEIR LIVES!
I OFFER YOU LENIENCY, PRISONERS! EXPLAIN YOUR MISSION HERE, AND I WILL ALLOW YOU TO DIE PAINLESSLY!

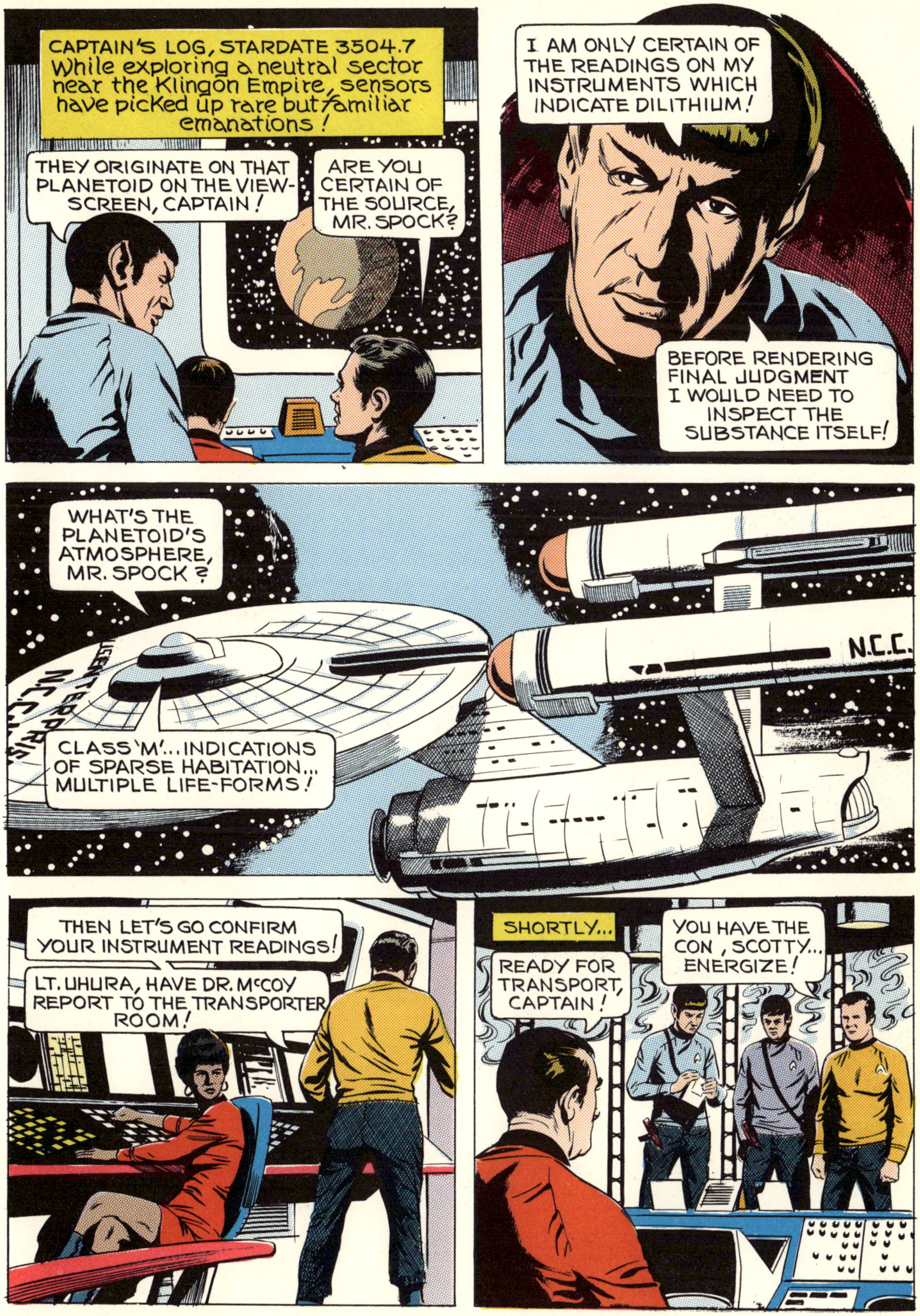

WHAT'S THE PLANETOID'S ATMOSPHERE, MR. SPOCK?

CLASS 'M'... INDICATIONS OF SPARSE HABITATION... MULTIPLE LIFE-FORMS!

N.C.C.

THEN LET'S GO CONFIRM YOUR INSTRUMENT READINGS!

LT. UHURA, HAVE DR. McCOY REPORT TO THE TRANSPORTER ROOM!

SHORTLY...

READY FOR TRANSPORT, CAPTAIN!

YOU HAVE THE CON, SCOTTY... ENERGIZE!

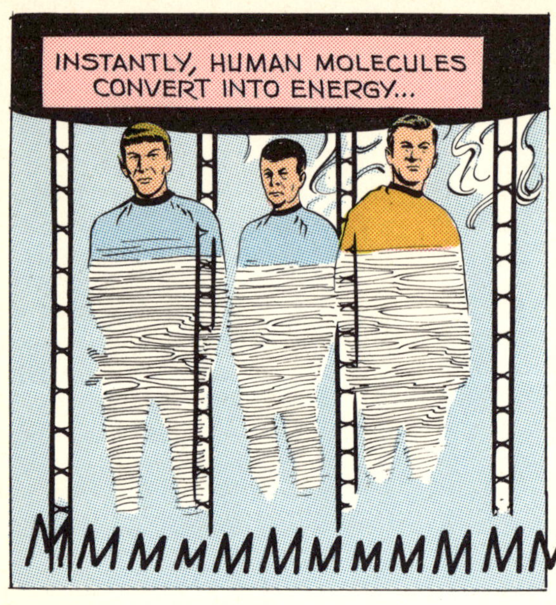
INSTANTLY, HUMAN MOLECULES CONVERT INTO ENERGY...
MMMMMMMMMMMMMM

AND REASSEMBLE ON THE SURFACE OF THE ALIEN WORLD!
MMMMMMMMMMMMMMMM.....

IF THE REST OF THE WORLD IS LIKE THIS BARREN TERRAIN I CAN'T SEE IT SUPPORTING LIFE!
NEVERTHELESS, I DETECT A SMALL POCKET OF LIVING BEINGS!

THEY REGISTER IN THE SAME AREA AS THE DILITHIUM READINGS!
HOW MUCH DILITHIUM, SPOCK? IS IT WORTH BRINGING IN A MINING CREW?
SLOW DOWN, BONES! BEFORE WE MINE ANYTHING, WE'VE GOT TO FIND OUT HOW THE INHABIT-ANTS FEEL ABOUT IT!
SORRY, JIM...IT'S JUST THAT I KNOW HOW VALUABLE THE STUFF IS!

SO DO I! WITHOUT DILITHIUM THERE'D BE NO STARSHIPS! STILL WE CAN'T JUST MOVE IN AND HELP OURSELVES WHEREV...

AHHH
NNN
NNNN

A JOLTING SHOCK... NUMBING DARKNESS... THEN NOTHINGNESS, UNTIL...
WHAT...WHAT HAPPENED?

TO INVOKE AN ANCIENT EARTH EXPRESSION, WE HAVE BEEN AMBUSHED... BY **KLINGONS**!
CORRECT! AND IF YOU TRY TO RESIST, OUR PHASERS ARE NOW SET TO DISINTEGRATE!

YOU MUST KNOW, LIEUTENANT, THAT THIS ATTACK IS A VIOLATION OF THE TREATY BETWEEN THE FEDERATION AND THE KLINGON EMPIRE!
NOT AT ALL! WE ARE MERELY BENDING THE TREATY A BIT! YOU WILL BE RELEASED AT THE PROPER TIME!

APPARENTLY, THEY WISH ONLY TO DELAY US, NOT HARM US!
BUT THEY TOOK OUR PHASERS... WE'RE HELPLESS!
NOT NECESSARILY, BONES!

THEY LEFT YOU WITH YOUR MEDICAL KIT... AND I THINK I'M WOUNDED!
GOTCHA, JIM!

WAIT! WHAT ARE YOU REACHING FOR, DOCTOR?
MY SPRAY APPLICATOR! THE CAPTAIN CUT HIMSELF WHEN HE FELL!

CUT HIMSELF? WHERE? I SEE **NOTHING**!

YI-I-I-I-I
NOW YOU DO!

SMACK

A DEFT VULCAN NERVE PINCH...

YAAA
UH-H-H

COME ON... THIS PATH MUST LEAD SOME-WHERE!

THOSE WOULD BE SOME OF THE PLANETOID'S INHABITANTS, NO DOUBT!
AS I FEARED, THEY'VE GOT VISITORS! A KLINGON WARSHIP COMMANDER AND HIS PARTY!

AH!...VISITORS FROM THE FEDERATION! YOU ARE TOO LATE, GENTLEMEN!
TOO LATE... FOR WHAT?

I ASSUME YOU HAVE COME FOR THE DILITHIUM, CAPTAIN! BUT THIS TREATY GIVES EXCLU-SIVE MINING RIGHTS TO THE KLINGON EMPIRE!

TREATY... WITH WHOM?
I, THE GRAND QAAL OF EULUS, HAVE BESTOWED UPON THEM SUCH RIGHTS!

THIS SUBSTANCE, WHICH YOU CALL DILITHIUM, ABOUNDS ON OUR WORLD...
BUT IT IS OF NO USE TO US! THE KLINGONS ARE WELCOME TO IT!

BUT, YOU DON'T UNDER-STAND! THE KLINGONS ARE A WARLIKE PEOPLE! THEY'LL USE THE DILITHIUM FOR CONQUEST, AND SUBJUGATION!
WE ON EULUS CARE NAUGHT ABOUT YOUR PETTY RIVALRIES!

HAD YOU OF THE FEDERATION ARRIVED FIRST, OUR TREATY WOULD HAVE BEEN WITH YOU!
BUT NOW, THE DEED IS DONE... AND CANNOT BE UNDONE!

CAN'T IT? THAT TREATY BECAME INVALID THE MOMENT YOUR MEN WAYLAID US, COMMANDER!
WAYLAID YOU? CAN YOU PROVE THAT CAPTAIN? HOW DO I KNOW THAT YOU DID NOT WAYLAY **THEM?**

I SUGGEST, CAPTAIN, THAT YOU ADMIT DEFEAT GRACEFULLY!
COMMANDER TO ECTACUS... TRANSPORT TWO!

WHEN THEY RETURN, IT'LL BE WITH HEAVY MINING EQUIPMENT! I'M AFRAID WE REALLY LOST THIS ROUND!
CRZZZAP

NOT NECESSARILY, CAPTAIN!
WHAT DO YOU MEAN, SPOCK?

ACCORDING TO THE FINE READINGS ON MY TRICORDER, THE MOLECULES OF THAT DILITHIUM ARE IN A CONSTANT STATE OF FLUX!

ARE YOU SURE?...I MEAN, DILITHIUM IS THE MOST RIGID SUBSTANCE KNOWN!
IN ITS NATURAL STATE, YES...BUT NOT IF IT WERE SYNTHESIZED OR, WORSE STILL, MANUFACTURED!

MANUFACTURED? DILITHIUM?
JIM...THERE'S SOMETHING ELSE STRANGE GOING ON HERE!

WHAT LITTLE SURPRISE ARE **YOU** ABOUT TO SPRING, BONES?
ACCORDING TO MY HEARTBEAT READER, THERE'S AN IMPOSTOR AMONG US!

WHAT'S MORE, WHO-EVER HE IS, HIS READOUT REGISTERS **EARTH HUMAN**!

AN EARTHMAN... HERE ?... CAN YOU FERRET HIM OUT, BONES ?
I ALREADY HAVE, JIM! OBVIOUSLY, HE ISN'T ONE OF THESE... HOWEVER...

SYNTHETIC DILITHIUM... AN IMPOSTOR FROM EARTH... THE GAME IS OVER, MR. GRAND QAAL!
I... UH... KNOW NOT OF WHAT YOU SPEAK!

DON'T YOU ? I'D BET MY COMMISSION THAT WHEN I PEEL AWAY THIS HOOD, I'LL REVEAL...

HARRY MUDD!... ARCH THIEF, LIAR AND CON MAN EXTRAORDINARY!
END OF PART I

UHURA'S CROSSWORD

ACROSS

1. Captain of the Enterprise.
2. A light table with balls.
6. Heats the Earth.
7. Ancient South American Indian tribe.
8. Let It --.
9. James Bond is a well known one.
11. The front half of the spaceship.
15. In space you travel a long way to reach it.
16. --- and heir.
18. Enigmatic member of the crew — not all human.
20. Poem.
21. What happens to every good thing.

DOWN

1. Mortal enemies of the Enterprise's crew.
2. Old train travels through space.
3. Felt at the wrist with your finger on it.
4. Opposite of 'off'.
5. Not the truth.
8. Next to.
10. Place of detention.
12. Half a neck.
13. A walk through the stars.
14. Enterprise's doctor — skin as well!
17. Definately not even.
19. Do this -- else!

12 DIFFERENCES BETWEEN THE ABOVE TWO PICTURES

ANSWERS:

1. PLANET BY CPN. KIRK'S EYE
2. ROCKET STREAM UNDER SPOCK'S CHIN
3. 4TH PLANET HOP
4. PLANET IN ELECTRIC STORM (BOTTOM HALF)
5. PART OF STORM
6. SPOCK'S EYEBROW SHORTER
7. LINES ON PLANET IN CENTRE
8. WINDOWS ON 'ENTERPRIZE'
9. NOTCHES ON DIAL (INSTRUMENT PANEL)
10. INSTRUMENT CONSUL
11. BACK OF CHAIR (FAR RIGH
12. STAR AT TOP OF PIC.

COLOUR IN ALL
THE SHAPES WITH
A SPOT AND THE
ENTERPRIZE WILL APPEAR

STAR TREK

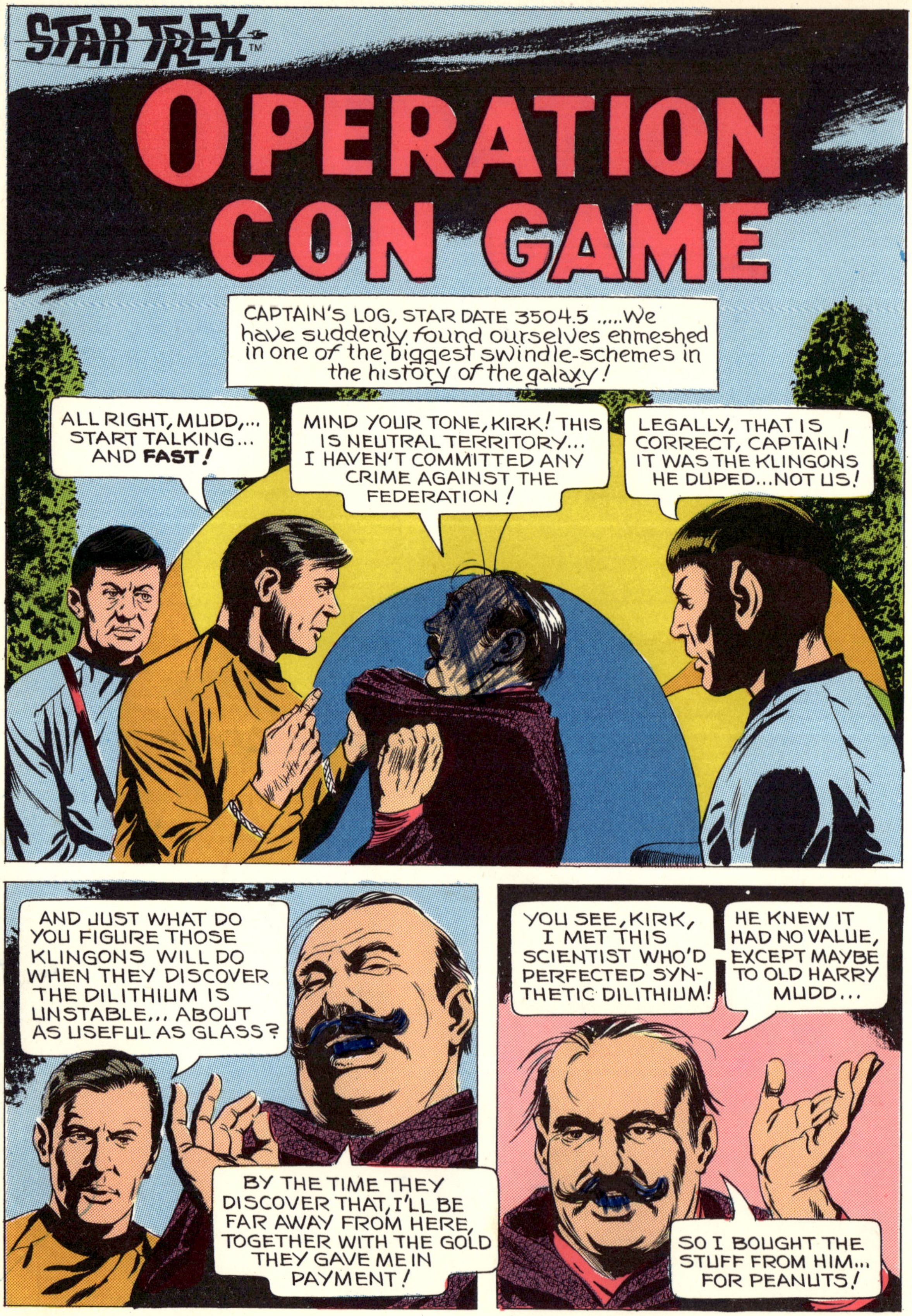

STAR TREK™

OPERATION CON GAME

CAPTAIN'S LOG, STAR DATE 3504.5 .....We have suddenly found ourselves enmeshed in one of the biggest swindle-schemes in the history of the galaxy!

ALL RIGHT, MUDD,... START TALKING... AND **FAST**!

MIND YOUR TONE, KIRK! THIS IS NEUTRAL TERRITORY... I HAVEN'T COMMITTED ANY CRIME AGAINST THE FEDERATION!

LEGALLY, THAT IS CORRECT, CAPTAIN! IT WAS THE KLINGONS HE DUPED...NOT US!

I SET UP SHOP HERE BECAUSE I KNEW KLINGON SHIPS PATROL THE VICINITY!
AND THESE PRIMITIVE NATIVES MADE PERFECT "SUBJECTS" FOR THE "GRAND QAAL"!

NOW, I'LL JUST TAKE MY GOLD AND BE ON MY WAY!
YOU CAN HAVE THIS DILITHIUM, KIRK, AS A KEEPSAKE!

KWUUM

WH...WHAT HAPPENED?
YOU TELL US, MUDD?

INTERESTING... BECAUSE OF ITS FLUID MOLECULAR STRUCTURE, THIS SUBSTANCE IS EASILY EXPLODED!
N-NOBODY EVER TOLD ME THAT! I COULD'VE... ≥GULP≤ BEEN KILLED!!

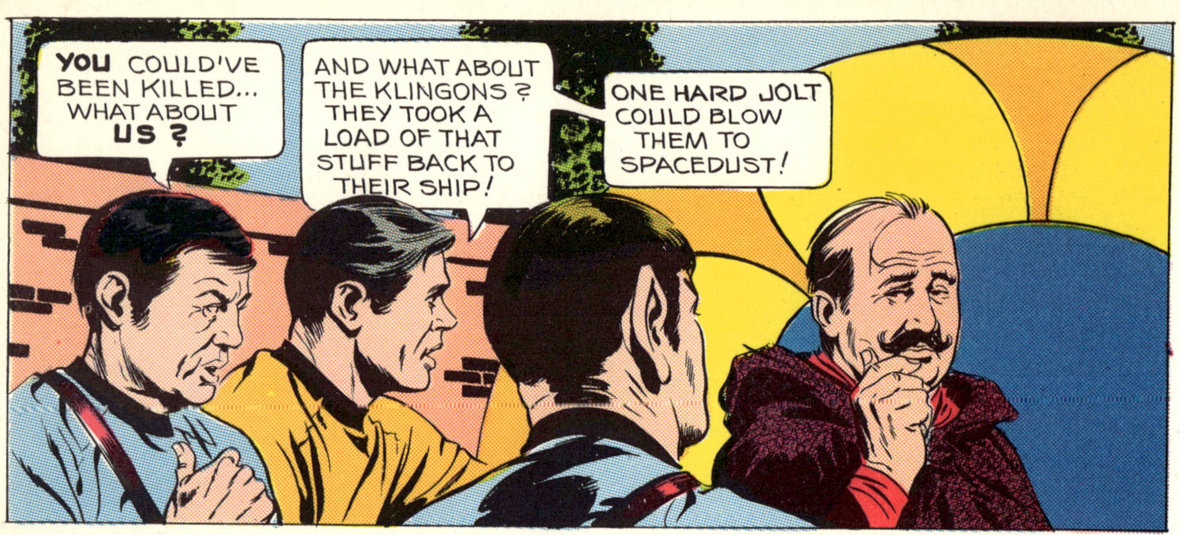
YOU COULD'VE BEEN KILLED... WHAT ABOUT US ?
AND WHAT ABOUT THE KLINGONS ? THEY TOOK A LOAD OF THAT STUFF BACK TO THEIR SHIP!
ONE HARD JOLT COULD BLOW THEM TO SPACEDUST!

WHY... THAT WOULD MAKE ME A HERO! IMAGINE... WIPING OUT A KLINGON WARSHIP... SINGLE-HANDED!
OH-H-H ??...AND WHAT ABOUT THE FULL-SCALE WAR THAT WOULD START BETWEEN THE KLINGONS AND THE FEDERATION!

SPOCK, CONTACT THE KLINGONS AND WARN THEM ABOUT THE...
I HAVE ALREADY TRIED, CAPTAIN, AND FAILED! BEING DISTRUSTFUL BY NATURE, THE KLINGONS BELIEVE MY WARNING IS SOME SORT OF RUSE!

THEN THERE'S ONLY ONE THING TO DO! BONES, DO YOU THINK YOU CAN HANDLE MUDD BY YOURSELF ?
WHY NOT ? EVEN SHIPS' DOCTORS HAVE TAKEN SOME COMBAT TRAINING!

WHAT ARE THOSE THREE SCHEMING ? WHATEVER IT IS, THEY'RE NOT OUT-SMARTIN' HARRY MUDD...
I STILL GOT A FEW ACES UP MY SLEEVE!

KIRK TO ENTERPRISE... TWO FOR TRANSPORT!
TWO...?

MMMMMMMMMMMMMM
WH...WHY ARE THEY LEAVING YOU HERE?
TO WATCH YOU, MUDD!
MAYBE WE CAN'T ARREST YOU, BUT WE CAN AT LEAST MAKE SURE YOU DON'T CAUSE ANY MORE MISCHIEF!

...AND LORD KNOWS, YOU'VE ALREADY CAUSED PLENTY!
BECAUSE OF YOU, THERE'S ONLY ONE WAY TO PROTECT THE KLINGONS FROM YOUR PHONY DILITHIUM!

TRANSPORT YE ABOARD THE KLINGON CRAFT? CAPTAIN, YE MUST BE JOKIN'!
I WAS NEVER MORE SERIOUS, SCOTTY!

FIX ON SOME UNMANNED AREA... LIKE ONE OF THEIR HOLDS...AND REMAIN ON THOSE COORDINATES TILL MY NEXT TRANSMISSION!
AYE, AYE, SIR... BUT IF YE DON'T MIND MY SAYIN' SO, IT'S SHEER MADNESS!

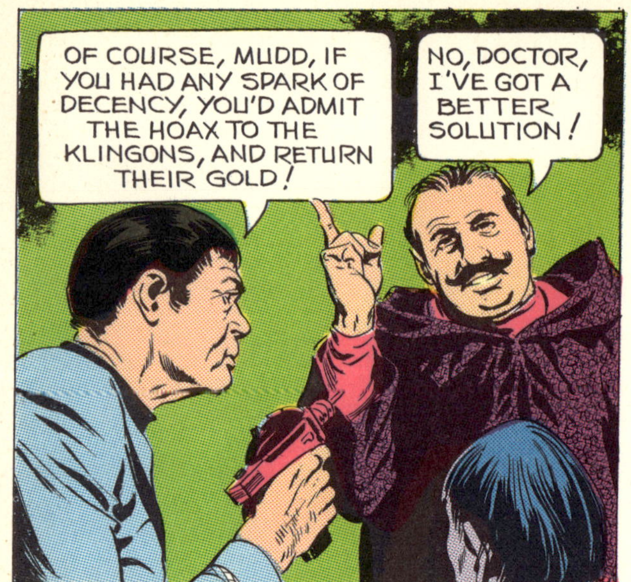
OF COURSE, MUDD, IF YOU HAD ANY SPARK OF DECENCY, YOU'D ADMIT THE HOAX TO THE KLINGONS, AND RETURN THEIR GOLD!
NO, DOCTOR, I'VE GOT A BETTER SOLUTION!

WHAT ARE YOU UP TO NOW?
EVER SINCE I MASTERED THESE NATIVES' SIGN-LANGUAGE, THEY'VE WORSHIPPED ME! THEY'LL DO WHAT-EVER I SAY!

LIKE TAKING YOU **PRISONER**!

AT THE SAME TIME, ABOARD THE KLINGON SHIP...
WHICH DIRECTION, SPOCK?
THERE IS ONLY ONE LOGICAL CHOICE, CAPTAIN!

THE PAIR MOVE CAUTIOUSLY ALONG A DIMLY LIT CORRIDOR...
BASED ON MY TRICORDER READINGS, AND IF MY MEMORY OF KLINGON WARSHIPS SERVES ME CORRECTLY, THE MAKE-SHIFT DILITHIUM IS IN THE CAPTAIN'S QUARTERS!

ONCE MY "SUBJECTS" LOAD THE GOLD ONTO MY SPACE-BUGGY, YOU AND ME ARE TAKING A LITTLE TRIP, DOCTOR!
WHERE TO, MR. MUDD?

SOME PLACE WHERE I CAN LOSE YOU...FOREVER! AFTER ALL, YOU'RE THE ONLY REMAINING WITNESS TO MY LITTLE, UH... TRANSACTION!
OH?...WHAT ABOUT CAPTAIN KIRK AND MR. SPOCK?

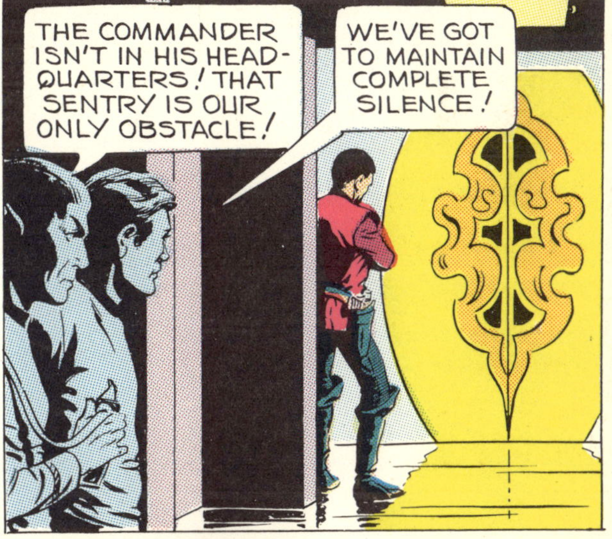
THE COMMANDER ISN'T IN HIS HEAD-QUARTERS! THAT SENTRY IS OUR ONLY OBSTACLE!
WE'VE GOT TO MAINTAIN COMPLETE SILENCE!

UH-H-H

IF WE WORK QUICKLY, WE CAN BE GONE BEFORE HE IS DISCOVERED!

THE KLINGONS AREN'T ALTOGETHER STUPID, YOU KNOW... THEY GAVE ME THIS TRANSMITTER IN CASE TROUBLE SHOULD DEVELOP!

THIS IS THE GRAND QAAL! THE MEN FROM THE FEDERATION PLAN TO INVADE YOUR CRAFT... THEY SEEK THE DILITHIUM!

THIS APPEARS TO BE THE ENTIRE QUANTITY!
GOOD! GRAB THE CONTAINER AND LET'S GET OUT...

BWEEOO-BWEEOOO
INVASION ALERT!

BWEEOOO-BWEEOOO-BWEEOOO
KIRK TO ENTERPRISE... TWO...
COMPLETE THAT TRANSMISSION AND YOU'RE BOTH **DEAD MEN!**

WHAT HAPPENED, MR. SCOTT?
BLAST IT, I CAN'T TELL! SUDDENLY HE WAS JUST... CUT OFF!

FAREWELL, MY SUBJECTS... HA-HA...IT'S BEEN NICE KNOWING YOU!

NOW LET'S SEE... WHERE SHOULD I DEPOSIT YOU, DOCTOR? SOME ISOLATED WORLD, I SUPPOSE, OFF THE BEATEN SPACE-PATH, WHERE YOU'RE NOT LIKELY **EVER** TO BE FOUND!

AS FOR ME... WITH ALL THIS GOLD, I MAY EVEN GO INTO RETIREMENT! HA, HA... IMAGINE HARRY MUDD LEADING THE LIFE OF AN HONEST MAN...

WHO WOULD BELIEVE IT? A FEDERATION CAPTAIN AND HIS FIRST OFFICER WALKED RIGHT INTO MY HANDS! THIS IS INDEED A GLORIOUS DAY!

THE TRUTH NOW, CAPTAIN! WHY DID YOU INVADE MY CRAFT?...SURELY IT WASN'T FOR THIS SMALL AMOUNT OF DILITHIUM!
WE TRIED TELLING YOU BEFORE, COMMANDER, BUT YOU WOULDN'T BELIEVE US!

OH, YES...SOME NONSENSE ABOUT IT BEING EXPLOSIVE!
MOVE! A FEW MINUTES IN OUR INTERROGATION CHAMBER SHOULD WRING OUT YOUR TRUE MOTIVES!

GET READY, CAPTAIN...

WHOOM

SMACK

SPOCK TO ENTERPRISE... TWO FOR TRANSPORT... NOW!

IN THE NEXT INSTANT...
CAPTAIN! WHAT IN BLAZES IS HAPPENIN'? I'VE LOST CONTACT WITH DR. McCOY!
WHAT??
INTERESTING! HARRY MUDD MUST HAVE OVERCOME HIM!

THAT ASTEROID SHOULD DO FINE, DOCTOR... IT'S NOT INCLUDED ON ANY STAR CHARTS!

TRACTOR BEAM LOCKED ON TARGET, CAPTAIN!
GOOD! TOW IT IN!

SUDDENLY...
RMM-RMM
SOMETHING'S WRONG! I CAN'T CONTROL THE SHIP'S COURSE

OH, NO! WE'RE BEING DRAWN BACK TO THE ENTERPRISE!
N.C.C.-1701

AND SO, A SHORT TIME LATER...
THAT'S THE LAST OF THE GOLD HE WAS CARRYIN', CAPTAIN!
ALL RIGHT, SCOTTY... ENERGIZE!

AFTERWARD...
WE THANK YOU FOR THE RETURN OF OUR GOLD, CAPTAIN! AS FOR THE DILITHIUM, YOU CONVINCED US OF ITS DEADLY NATURE, AND WE DISCARDED IT!

IN VIEW OF THE FACT THAT YOU MAY HAVE SAVED OUR LIVES, I WILL OVERLOOK YOUR CRIMINAL INVASION OF MY SHIP!
WHY, HOW GENEROUS OF YOU, COMMANDER! AS WE SAY ON MY NATIVE PLANET, YOU'RE ALL HEART!

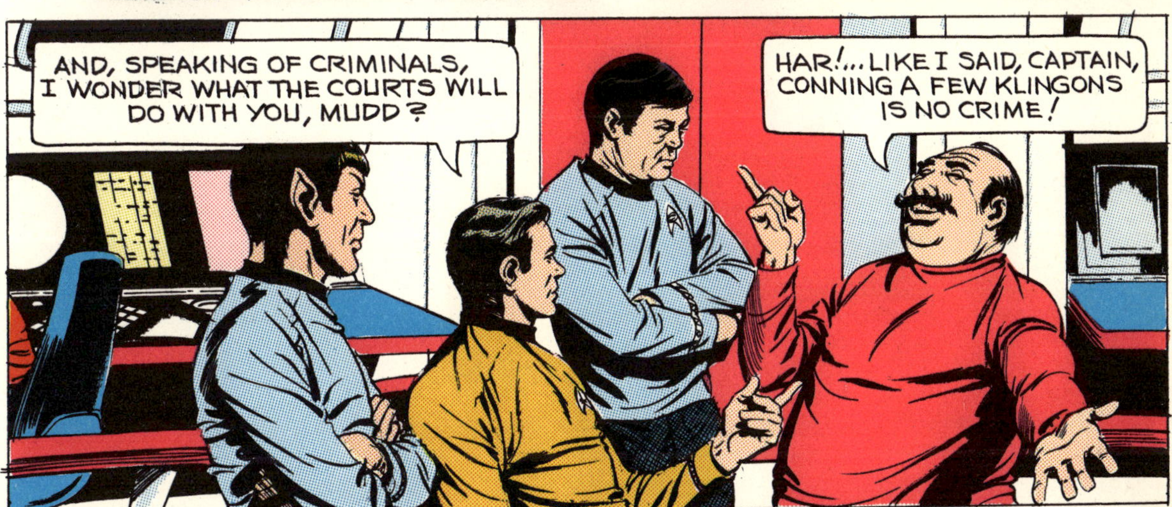
AND, SPEAKING OF CRIMINALS, I WONDER WHAT THE COURTS WILL DO WITH YOU, MUDD?
HAR!... LIKE I SAID, CAPTAIN, CONNING A FEW KLINGONS IS NO CRIME!

TRUE... BUT JEOPARDIZING TWO STARSHIP PERSONNEL... AND KIDNAPPING ANOTHER, SHOULD NET YOU A LONG, LONG SENTENCE!

DOCTOR, WOULD YOU CARE TO ESCORT THE PRISONER TO THE BRIG?
WITH EXTREME PLEASURE, CAPTAIN!
THE END

NSWERS
USS ENTERPRISE
NCC-170
UHURA'S CROSSWORD
KIRK POOL
L O SUN I
INCA L BE
N K SPY
G ENTER B
OUTER I O
N E SON
SPOCK ODE
R ENDS
WORDSEARCH ANSWER : BONES MCCOY

NCC-1701